The Jokers

by Chris Inns

F
FRANCES LINCOLN
CHILDREN'S BOOKS

Mungo the Elephant and Mr Thunderpants
loved playing jokes on each other...

For Joseph Francis Inns

First published in Great Britain and the USA in 2005 by
Frances Lincoln Children's Books, 4 Torriano Mews,
Torriano Avenue, London NW5 2RZ
www.franceslincoln.com

Distributed in the USA by Publishers Group West

First paperback edition published in Great Britain and the USA in 2006.

British Library Cataloguing in Publication Data available on request

ISBN 10: 1-84507-429-7
ISBN 13: 978-1-84507-429-6

The illustrations are acrylic and crayon

Printed in China

1 3 5 7 9 8 6 4 2

and they loved playing jokes
on their friends.

put itching powder
in Big Bear's cave,

scritch

scratch

I'll get those
cheeky monkeys!

left trick blue soap
in Lily's bathroom,

Hurrumph!

Sssave me!

and even put sneezing
powder into Mr Legg's
hat. He sneezed so
much he tied himself
into a knot!

But their friends
didn't always find
the jokes so funny.

One day their friend Lily came to ask them to her dressing-up party. Lily said there was going to be a prize for the silliest costume.

Mungo &
Mr Thunderpants
please come to
my party
from Lily x

Lily said she was going as a pirate queen...

Dawg was going as a spaceman,

The beagle has landed.

I grant you three wishes.

ppear as a fairy godmother,

and Mr Legg was going as a cowboy.

Yee Haa!

ssstick 'em up!

Mungo and Mr Thunderpants imagined how their friends would look in their funny costumes.

Lily hoped they would make an effort with their costumes.

Mungo and Mr Thunderpants decided that they would make themselves the best costumes ever and win the prize.

They worked hard all afternoon so that their costumes would be ready in time for the party.

They measured,

and cut,

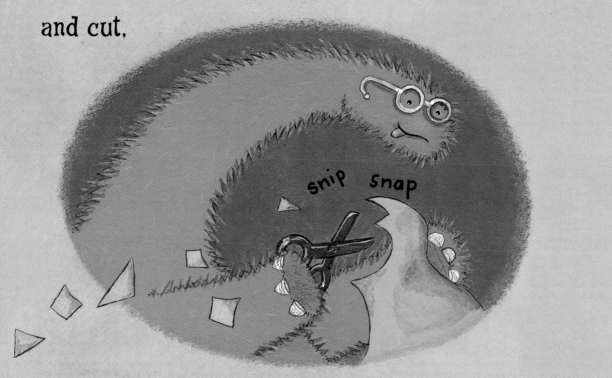

and glued,

and stitched,

until, at last, their costumes were finished.

They quickly got dressed...

and set off for Lily's party.

When they got to Lily's house
they burst in through the door.

But the surprise...

No one else was wearing a costume. It was a joke.
Their friends had got their own back.
Everybody laughed - even
the two jokers!

The party was the best ever - with dancing, games and fantastic party bags. Mungo and Mr Thunderpants clowned around and made everybody laugh.

And they promised not to play any more naughty jokes on their friends...

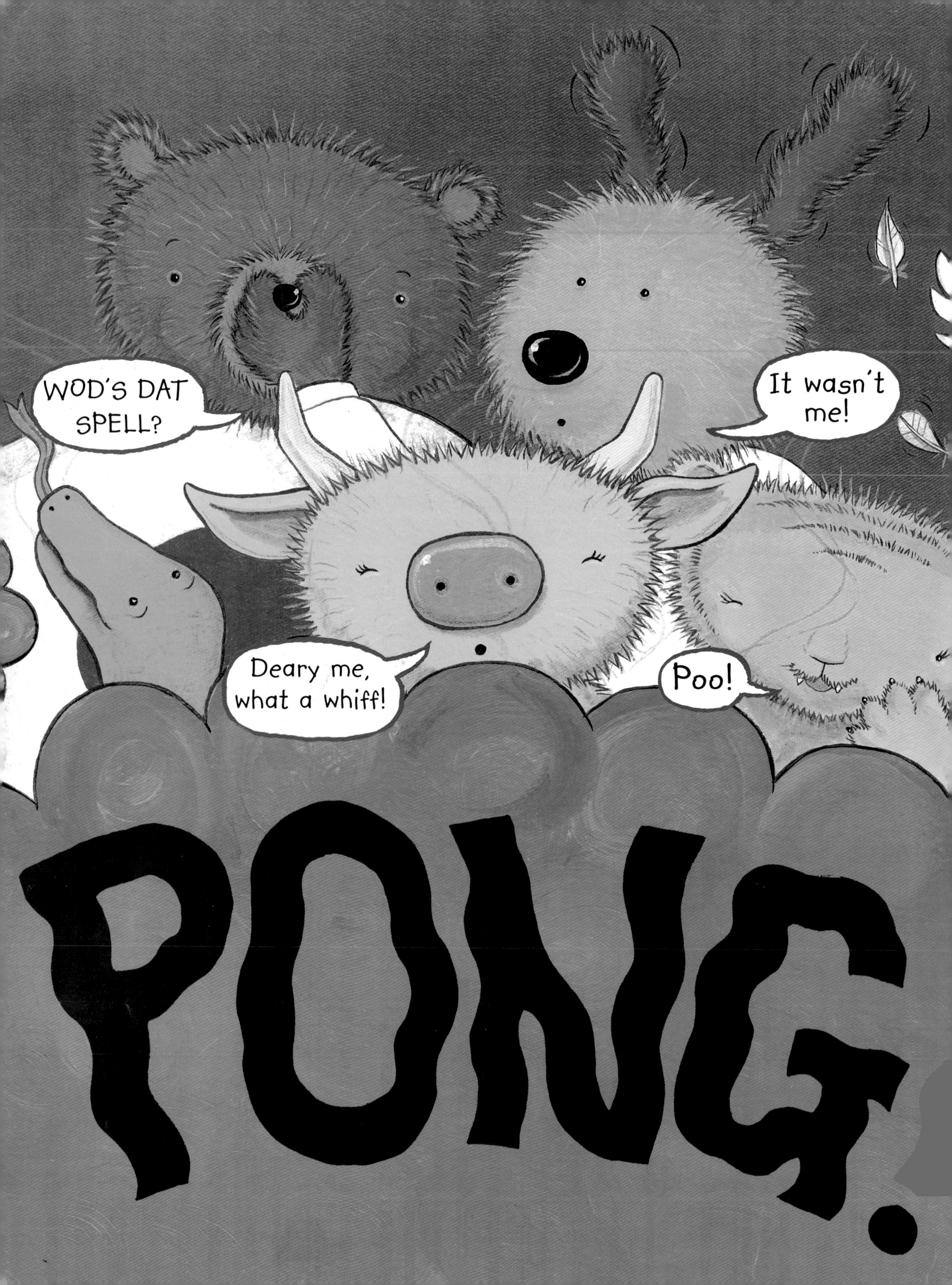
WOD'S DAT SPELL?
It wasn't me!
Deary me, what a whiff!
Poo!
PONG!

FURTHER TITLES AVAILABLE FROM
FRANCES LINCOLN CHILDREN'S BOOKS

NEXT!
Christopher Inns

Come and visit the toy hospital! Doctor Hopper
and Nurse Rex Barker are very busy today.
There are lots of sick toys, all waiting their turn to
be called in when Doctor Hopper shouts..."NEXT!"

ISBN-10: 0-7112-1697-5 (UK only)
ISBN-13: 978-0-7112-1697-6 (UK only)

HELP!
Christopher Inns

There is no time to rest when you are on call at
the toy hospital. Doctor Hopper and Nurse Rex Barker have
to be ready for every emergency. You never know when they might
have to jump into their ambulance, or when they will hear a toy
in trouble on the radio, shouting... "HELP!"

ISBN-10: 1-84507-123-9
ISBN-13: 978-1-84507-123-3

FANCY THAT!
Gillian Lobel
Illustrated by Adrienne Geoghegan

When Mother Crane discovers a nest of beautiful eggs
lying in the sand all alone, she decides to hatch them herself –
but what kind of babies will hatch out of them?
The other animals are sure that they have the answer
to the riddle, but when the babies start hatching and
calling for their mother, everyone gets a big surprise!

ISBN-10: 1-84507-335-5
ISBN-13: 978-1-84507-335-0

Frances Lincoln titles are available from all good bookshops.
You can also buy books and find out more about your favourite titles,
authors and illustrators on our website: www.franceslincoln.com